| | DATE DUE | |
|---|---|---|
| | | |
| | | |
| | | |
| | | |
| | | |
| | | |
| | | |
| | | |
| | | |
| | | |

To my son, Benny, and my daughter, Ruby,
who are just as sweet awake as they are asleep

Requests for permission to make copies of any part of the work should be mailed to the following address:
Permissions Department, Harcourt, Inc., 6277 Sea Harbor Drive, Orlando, Florida 32887-6777.

Excerpt from *These Boots Are Made for Walkin'*, written by Lee Hazlewood,
© 1965–'66/Renewed 1993–'94 Criterion Music Corp., reprinted by permission of Criterion Music Corporation.

Library of Congress Cataloging-in-Publication Data
Davis, Katie, 1959–
I hate to go to bed!/Katie Davis.
p.   cm.
Summary: Convinced that her parents are having a party after she goes to bed,
a little girl devises several plans to find out what she's missing.
ISBN 0-15-201920-0
[1. Bedtime—Fiction.   2. Dreams—Fiction.   3. Parent and child—Fiction.]   I. Title.
PZ7.D2944In   1999
[E]—dc21      98-22331

C  E  G  I  K  L  J  H  F  D
Printed in Singapore

The illustrations in this book were done
in acrylic paints and pen on hot press Arches watercolor paper.
The display type and text type were set in Heatwave.
Color separations by Bright Arts Graphics Pte. Ltd., Singapore
Printed and bound by Tien Wah Press, Singapore
Production supervision by Stanley Redfern
Designed by Linda Lockowitz

# I Hate to Go to Bed!

Written and illustrated by

## KATIE DAVIS

HARCOURT, INC.

San Diego   New York   London

I'm practically positive my parents are having a party,

even though they pretend like they're not.

I had to find out what I was missing.
So tonight at bedtime I came up with a plan.

I started acting really, really

*really sleepy.*

I waited until they thought I was fast asleep.

**Then I slipped out of bed.**

I was very quiet.

**But I got caught.**

"Go to bed!" Mommy said. "Go to bed!" Daddy said.

But I HATE to go to bed.

So I made a gigantic pair of binoculars to see what I was missing.

But by the time I got it all put together,

my parents were just sitting there. No party. No guests. Nothing.

"Go to bed!" Mommy said. "Go to bed!" Daddy said.

But I HATE to go to bed.

So I came up with another brilliant idea.

I acted very, very, *very* good. My parents didn't suspect a thing.

Then I got out of bed and pretended I wanted a drink of water.
I really just wanted a piece of cake from the party.

Only somehow they figured it out.

Luckily the water idea ended up being a two-part plan.

After drinking it, I got out of bed again
and said I had to go to the bathroom.

But they knew what I was up to.

Apparently the water trick had been done before.

"Go to bed!" Mommy said. "Go to bed!" Daddy said.

But I HATE to go to bed.

**So I hid.**

I'm a very good hider, and they never noticed me following them.

This was my big chance....

I knew it! There was Daddy in a costume!
And Mommy was putting up streamers!

Oh. Daddy was just wearing pj's.
And Mommy was only flossing.

I couldn't believe it. Nothing was happening!

"Go to bed!" Mommy said. "Go to bed!" Daddy said.
But I HATE to go to bed.

It was time for Plan Z.

I pulled my blanket close . . .

...and thought about presents and balloons and cakes and stuff.

I would have my *own* party!

The best party in the whole wide world.
A really, really, *really* fantastic party...

...in my dreams.